This book belongs to:

\_ \_ \_ \_ \_ \_ \_ \_ \_ \_ \_ \_

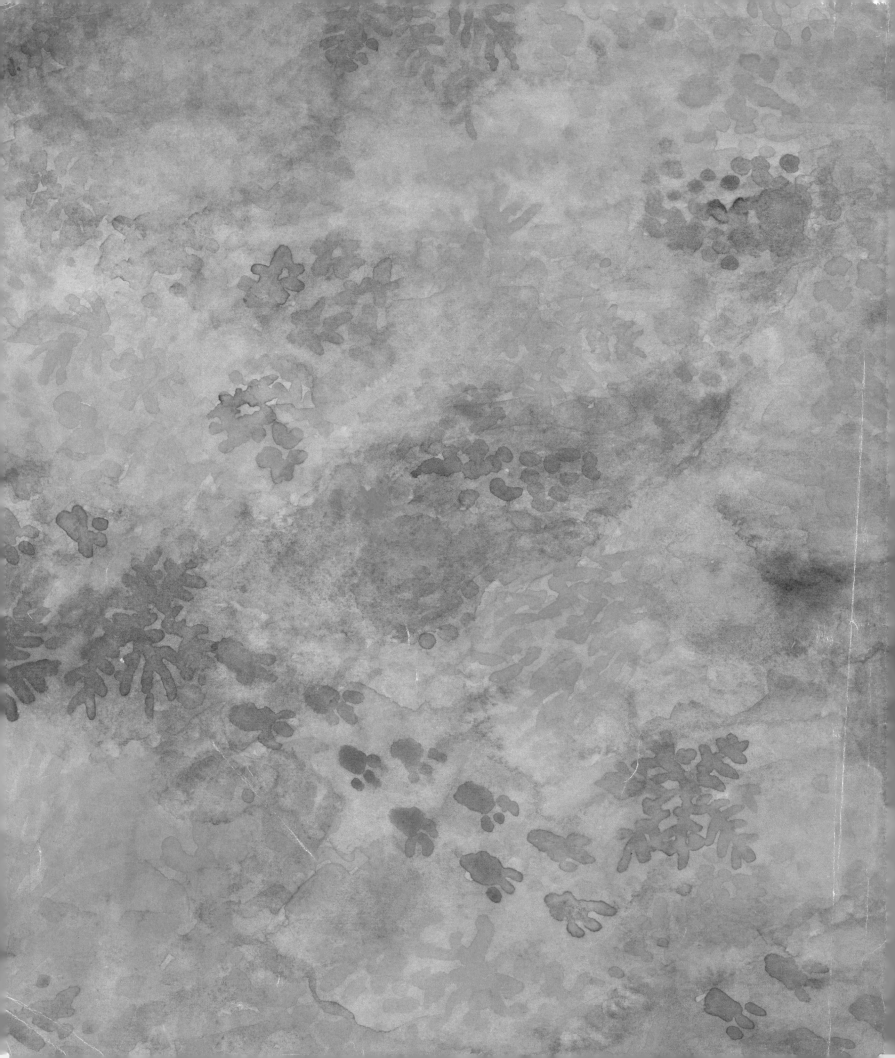

To
Freddie & Nell
With Love

First published in Great Britain in 2011 by Andersen Press Ltd.,

20 Vauxhall Bridge Road, London SW1V 2SA.

Published in Australia by Random House Australia Pty.,

Level 3, 100 Pacific Highway, North Sydney, NSW 2060.

Text and Illustration copyright © John Fardell, 2011

Colour separated in Switzerland by Photolitho AG, Zürich.

Printed and bound in Singapore by Tien Wah Press.

John Fardell has used pen, ink and watercolour in this book.

10    9    8    7    6    5    4    3    2

British Library Cataloguing in Publication Data available.

ISBN 978 1 84939 387 4

# THE DAY LOUIS GOT EATEN

## John Fardell

ANDERSEN PRESS

Louis and his big sister Sarah were out in the woods one day . . .

. . . when, unfortunately . . .

... Louis was eaten up by a Gulper.

Sarah didn't panic. She knew that Gulpers usually swallow their food down whole, and that if she was quick, there might be a way to get Louis back out.

Stopping only to collect something she thought she might need ...

...she set off after the Gulper in hot pursuit.

She had almost caught up with it when, unfortunately . . .

...the Gulper was eaten up by a Grabular.

Sarah followed the Grabular to its nest.

She had almost caught up with
it when, unfortunately ...

Sarah chased after the Undersnatch ...

...and had almost caught up with it ...

... when, unfortunately ...

...*it* was eaten up by a Spiney-backed Guzzler.

Sarah had almost caught up with the Spiney-backed Guzzler ...

... when, unfortunately ...

... *it* was eaten up by a Sabre-toothed Yumper.

Sarah chased after the Sabre-toothed Yumper ...

... and, fortunately, managed to track it to its lair,
without it being eaten up by anything.

She waited until it was asleep ...

... then crept up to its open mouth.

She crawled into its stomach . . .

. . . then clambered into the mouth of the Spiney-backed Guzzler . . .

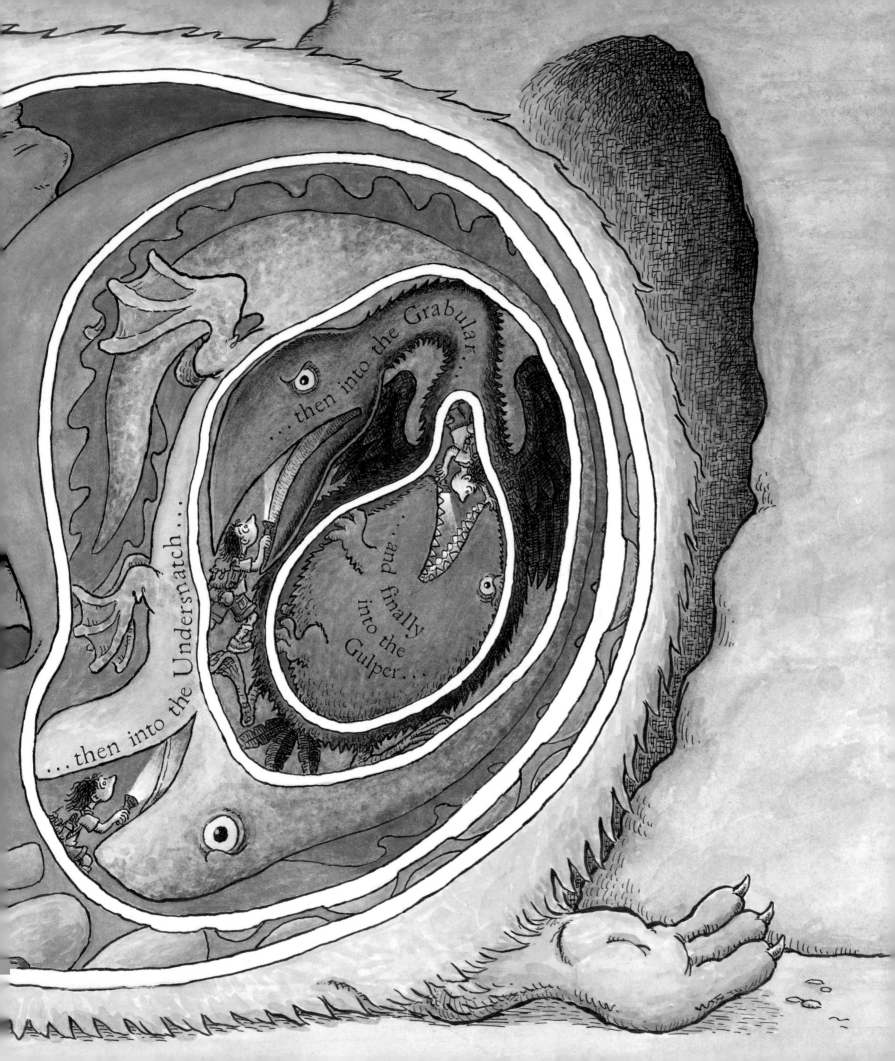

...where she found Louis.

"There you are," he said. "I knew you'd come. How are we going to get out of here?"

"We're going to use this Hiccup Frog," said Sarah, "which I picked up before chasing after the Gulper. Watch this."

The Hiccup Frog boinged all around the Gulper's stomach...

...which made the Gulper
start to wriggle.

This made the
Grabular wriggle,
which set off
the Undersnatch,
and then the
Spiney-backed Guzzler,
and then the
Sabre-toothed Yumper ...

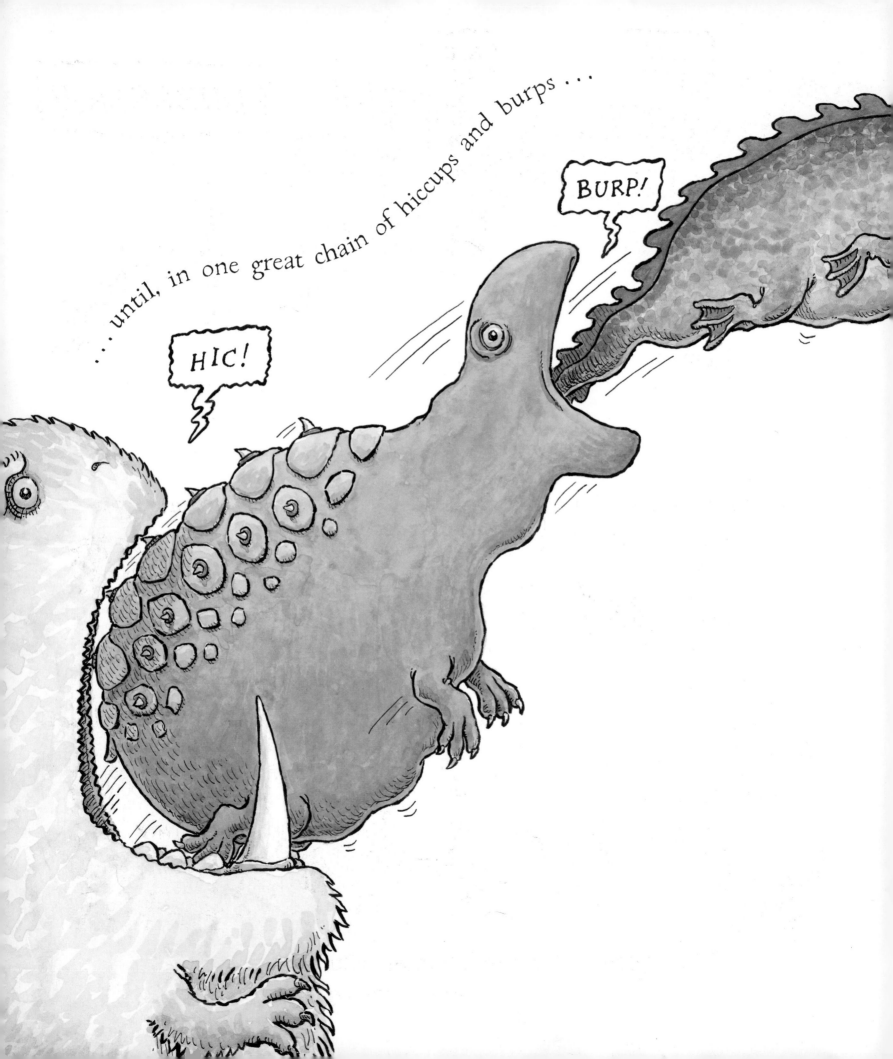

... Louis and Sarah (and the Hiccup Frog) were free.

Unfortunately, all the creatures were now extremely hungry.

They gathered around Sarah, licking their lips.

"GET AWAY FROM MY SISTER!"
shouted Louis. "OR I'LL **EAT YOU UP!**"

The creatures fled.

"Thanks, Louis," said Sarah.
"Come on, it's time to go home."

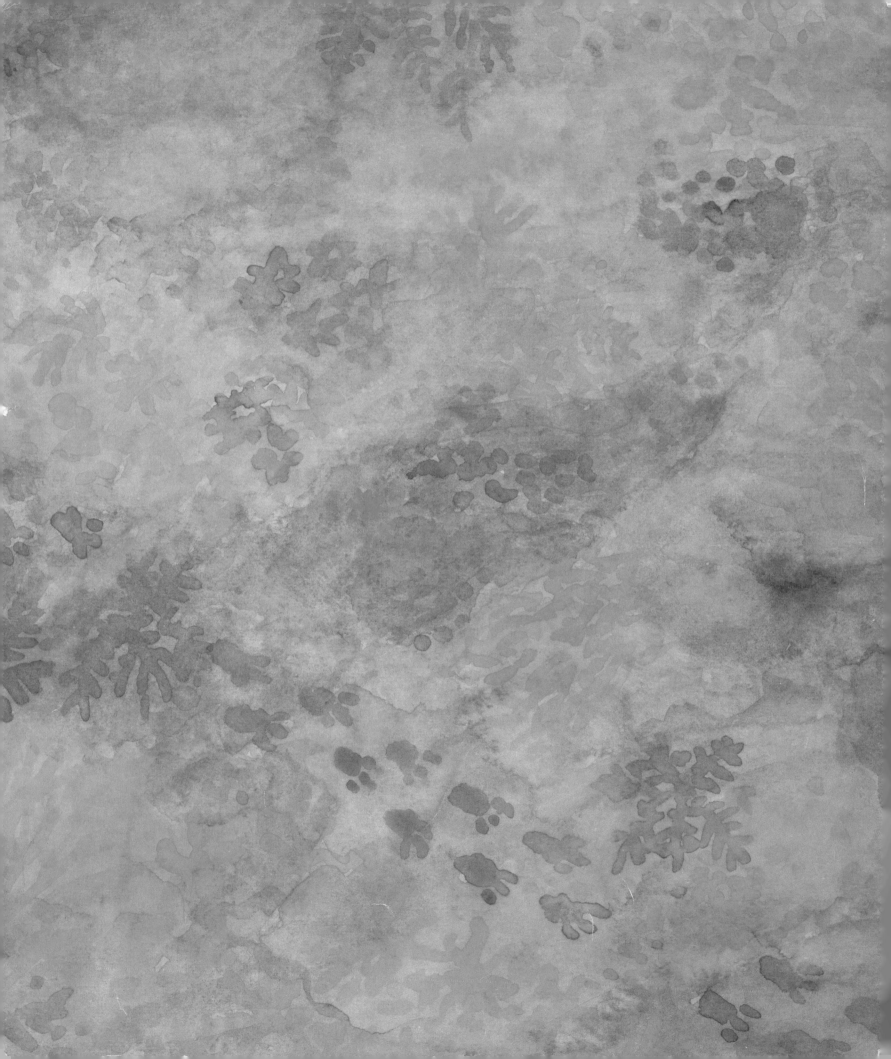

If you've enjoyed this, you'll love:

9781849391474

A recommended Children's Book of the Year - *TELEGRAPH*

SHORTLISTED FOR THE BOOKTRUST EARLY YEARS AWARD